SHACKLES
AND
WEBS

Mary Nelson

Illustrations by Andrew Hazel
Formatting of cover by Darees Nelson
Adinkra Symbols and meanings
www.welltempered.net/adinkra

1

We at Trafford believe that it is the responsibility of us all, as both individuals and corporations, to make choices that are environmentally and socially sound. You, in turn, are supporting this responsible conduct each time you purchase a Trafford book, or make use of our publishing services. To find out how you are helping, please visit www.trafford.com/responsiblepublishing.html

Our mission is to efficiently provide the world's finest, most comprehensive book publishing service, enabling every author to experience success. To find out how to publish your book, your way, and have it available worldwide, visit us online at www.trafford.com

Trafford rev. 6/19/2009

 www.trafford.com

North America & international
toll-free: 1 888 232 4444 (USA & Canada)
phone: 250 383 6864 ♦ fax: 250 383 6804 ♦ email: info@trafford.com

The United Kingdom & Europe
phone: +44 (0)1865 487 395 ♦ local rate: 0845 230 9601
facsimile: +44 (0)1865 481 507 ♦ email: info.uk@trafford.com

CONSTRUCT A STRUCTURE OF EQUALITY

Dedicated to my husband, our children, our families, friends and colleagues on all sides of the OLD TRIANGLE..

TOGETHER

We move forward to support each other in the building of the NEW LANDS, empowered by those who went before us.

The River

LEADING TO NEW HORIZONS

3

Shackles and Webs

SHACKLES AND WEBS

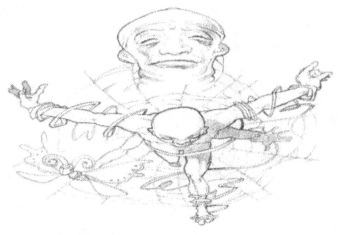

"The twisted tendrils he thought were constraining his limbs were the threads of the web spun by the spider and his forefathers revealing wisdom and creativity amongst the complexities of life."

INTRODUCTION

The 2007 bicentenary of the abolition of the Transatlantic Maafa* / Holocaust has revealed a landscape of complex issues impacting on beliefs and aspirations of all stakeholders.

*Swahili word meaning disaster, terrible occurrence or great tragedy.

5

'Shackles and Webs' uses narrative as a tool to uncover and confront the often uncomfortable issues that need to be faced by everyone whose journey through life has included the legacy and scars from the storms on the transatlantic journey. This could be as descendants of unwilling passengers; captains, masters or crew members; or as spectators.

In the story, Truth, portrayed as a butterfly, meets Kwaku Ananse,* the spider from Africa, whose creative escapades have travelled across time, oceans and continents to impact on many lives. The unique, creative being is sometimes a spider and sometimes a man. He adapts himself to reveal before our eyes a magical picture of the insignificant creature humiliating the larger one. This helps us to understand the outstanding bravery and creative survival tactics displayed along the continental passage and the transatlantic journeys. *From the Twi language meaning spider, born on a Wednesday.

During the journeys diverse tales merged through the interface of people from different places in Africa. Ananse modifies his image to deal with the new challenges confronting him and Tiger takes on the role of the oppressor. But the same messages of cleverness and resilience shine through as beacons of light with Ananse remaining as the key character.

In 'Shackles and Webs', the metamorphosis of the Ananse character takes another turn as he moves into today's world. He evolves from the loner

6

to work together with Truth and the Sankofa bird, based on the Adinkra symbol. In this new form, and well equipped from his past experiences, he is able to give guidance to other characters that are stuck in the midst of a tangled mix of issues and tensions, manipulated by Tiger. The Sankofa bird supports Ananse and Truth in their endeavours to deal with the past and helps others to move forward with a positive, creative frame of mind into the future.

This is graphically illustrated by the surreal appearance of the image of *465* at the beginning of the story, and at other moments when helplessness and despair strike a powerful blow.

Across the lands affected by the Transatlantic Maafa, different methods of marking slaves were used. Common to every situation was taking away the real name of the person, denying humanity and any ownership of previous history. They were classed as no more than property, to be dealt with as such and to profit none but the owners. The numbers *465* represent this image, displaying the worst crime against humanity we cannot ignore or ever forget.

But despite this recurring image, the key characters, based on real people's experiences, become powerfully enlightened by the unique encounters with Ananse, Truth and the Sankofa bird. They are then able to deal with obstacles along the way and remnants from history which, harmfully portrayed, have continued to trouble them. Secure in their identity, they confidently move forward to reach for their goals, and Tiger's selfish schemes are thwarted.

The cruel triangle was constructed at a time when diverse worlds were trying to connect. But it was built on a foundation of lies and greed, sustained by congruent walls of selfishness and ignorance, and upheld by angles of conformity. Lightening flashes of inhumanity and division continually penetrated the centre of the shambolic nightmare.

However, alongside this geometric disaster, new journeys can, and must be started by all who are willing to confront the wrongs of the atrocities. There then needs to be commitment to making sure they are not repeated; and for those who prospered then, and continue to prosper now from the Maafa, to do what is necessary to support the repair of the open wounds. We can all then begin moving forward to a future that empowers everyone equally; valuing the contributions that the current and upcoming generations can make together in our worlds yet to come.

Along with this there should be a sympathetic understanding of how cultural landscapes and individual mindsets were shaped by past experiences. This will enable us to build a new structure with a foundation of trust, supported by unity and reconciliation and empowered by wisdom, creativity and resourcefulness.

While new journeys are being started there must be an appreciation of the benefits for all in reconnecting our diverse worlds with this sound foundation. Following this there should be a dedication to the establishment of sustainable, joint enterprises with the lands that were a part of the old triangle. Then a rainbow will be able to shine through the dreams, embracing equality, hope and freedom, transforming them into a reality.

The experiences transcribed in the narrative endeavour to cover some of the many stories that can be told, but are in no way exhaustive.

It is important to understand that reading the story will also feel like a journey from the old to the new. The reader must persevere creatively, through the rough and smooth times, and then gaze at the rivers flowing down from the mountainous formation of the new structure, in the context of the source and the current landscapes, empowered and ready to plot new paths for the future.

On the landscapes of this formation the true stories must be told, the real heroes honoured and their legacy embraced by the various crowds on the horizon.

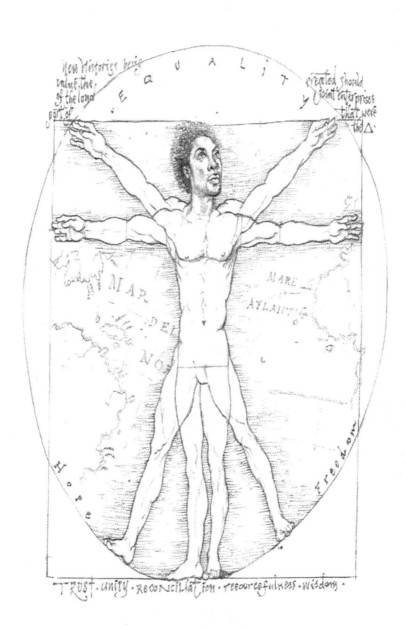

Shackles and Webs

SHACKLES AND WEBS

PART ONE

Shackles

The Golden Gate slammed shut again and _465_ looked to the sun rising on the horizon.

Trapped and lonely in his darkened corner, the shadows of depression hung like a banner over his fallen head. He tried to move his limbs, but after attempts too many to number he sighed in despair and the hazy horizon became a distant dream.

Fetters were twisted incessantly around his swollen ankles, repeatedly threading the number 8 in and out of the protruding bones. Burnished red drops trickled steadily from under them. Whilst pushing out his upper arms the pain intensified as he remembered the further fetters coiled around his neck and limbs.

Time was unknown. The relentless, darkened tunnel that had now become his mind loomed endlessly into the vacuum. His name and history had been gradually blotted from his memory as the journey through the tunnel continued.

He shut his eyes and slowly raised his head. In his mind a circle of light began to glow brightly. Within the circle an image of a ship appeared. He blinked and the shadow of a continent came alive. Africa flashed across the screen and he heard a voice call his name. Then it was gone and the darkness fell again.

From above, another force pulled at the strings manipulating him like a puppet. He followed the commands of the repeating rhythms.

"I'm coming, I will! I'm coming, I will! Yes Sir, Yes Sir, Yes!" His voice chimed like a broken bell being struck by flashes of lightening and his head lowered once more.

As if he was caught up in the storm, the low lying clouds hung around him, wrapped with heavy humidity and the lightning flashed like an angry whip.

"You will! You will! You will!!"

Days and years repeated in continuous rhythms of submission, the body now automatically continuing the beat of monotonous conformity. He raised his head and faked a smile as the flow became routine. The flashing lightening and the snap of the whip played together in orchestral harmony with conformity.

The spotlights blurred as the curtains slowly closed across the stage and the sound of silence replaced the beats of oppression.

Is this the only story.. story..story..story...?

The audience turned their heads as the silence was broken briefly by a mysterious growl. A shadow drifted through the air above them and sailed out of the door way.

PEMPAMSIE: Sew in readiness
Readiness, steadfastness, hardiness

Numerous decades rolled by like boulders, gathering residue in their path. In the background the heavy rhythms began to resonate again, breaking the silence.

The stage reopened in 1953, revealing Mr. Foster on his veranda in Jamaica, overlooking the foothills of the Blue Mountains. The branches of an orange tree provided the framework for the new scenery.

God save the Queen
"Sit up, walk straight, don't talk like that. Sit up, walk straight, don't talk like that. God save the Queen!"

He blinked his eyes and lifted his head up from the table where he had fallen asleep ....*465 465 465 465*....ran through his mind. He shook his head puzzled. Who was *465*? What had he been dreaming?

What about emancipation? Slavery was done a long time ago. He stood up straight, put his shoulders back, and sang out the National Anthem with pride. "God save our gracious Queen...."

A voice spoke to him from the shadows. "Come, we need help." His chance had come at last. "This way, a place is prepared for you; a better life is here for you." Then he remembered the stories he had heard about discoverers, heroes and writers from the Queen's land.

"We're coming," he answered.

Soon after, a ship was ploughing through the churning ocean carrying him and Mrs. Foster to another shore where he was told he was wanted. His brother's family chose to remain in Jamaica and they agreed to keep in touch as much as possible.

As the sun rose on the horizon of England, the promised Motherland, it blinked as if playing a tune with the continuing rhythm. Mr. Foster's eyes opened. He smiled, looking at the sun, and followed the rhythm of the crowd around him. They moved, he moved, they spoke, he spoke. He answered using the language that once pulled the strings. They smiled as he followed their leading on the road up to the Golden Gates.

"Stop! Go no further!" A strange, muffled voice commanded in the background. In the road loomed a massive gate that banged shut, driven by the aggressive breath of the Master.

Once more he was stopped, forced to obey, as he felt himself slammed back into the foreboding corner of despair. He worked around the clock to the rhythm of the ticks and the regular chimes that rang with a familiar cycle of obedience. The cycle continued as he climbed into his bed co-shared at the change of shifts as the sun rose each morning.

There were twelve of them in and out of that front door, sharing the pillows in between the exhaustive shifts that were as monotonous as life in

16

the fields of the past must have been.

"Five years," he sighed, "only five years and I'm going home with the money I've saved for my real freedom." With that hope in his mind, Mr. Foster settled to his work following the script before him.

He left the house one morning to find a new place to rest his head. The advertisement said, 'A nice one bedroom flat at a good price for an honest, hard working tenant.'

"That's me," he thought as he walked up to the door. The sign reached out to him as if the letters were alive, clawing at the air around him, 'NO COLOUREDS, NO DOGS!' He ran as if the dogs were chasing him back into his corner. There he sobbed!

As time passed he began to develop a growing resilience to the pressures around him. The road was long and hard but Mrs. Foster walked beside him. The children came along and the days moved on.

The savings grew slowly but the bills were high. Mr. Foster met regularly with others to gain strength to overcome the obstacles along the way. The Mother they had been lead to expect would welcome and support them seemed only to be pulling the strings.

Mr. Foster stood once more at the Golden Gates with his wife and children at his side. Staring sadly at the closed gates, he held on tightly to his family. Together they looked with anticipation at the lock on the golden frame.....

and sang…

"We shall overcome, we shall overcome,
We shall overcome some day.
Deep in my heart, I do believe,
We shall overcome some day."

ANANSE NTONTAN: Ananse's webs
Wisdom and creativity

The music faded and dense fog crept mysteriously through the bushes capturing the atmosphere around them. Time travelled on.

The Foster's children worked hard through their school years, and although many gates remained closed, they did not give up. Inspired by their parents determined vision they moved into adulthood and their own children arrived on the scene.

Mr. Foster had put the closed gates out of his mind until one day when everything seemed to have gone wrong. One of his grandsons had been in trouble at school for challenging the teacher in a history lesson about slavery. Money was short and bills were due. He had missed a call from his brother in Jamaica. Then suddenly he remembered that he had told him he was only coming to England for five years, and he had never been back home.

The scenery changed and the nightmare of the closed, locked gates came once more into Mr. Foster's mind. Memories of obstacles in the way of his vision when he had first travelled from Jamaica came rushing back. He felt himself isolated from his family and in the presence of *465* once more, smothered by a strange feeling of oppression all around him.

Without any warning the dense air was broken

by a solitary whistling sound. Mr. Foster saw a mysterious shadow rise over the gate.

He watched curiously as a butterfly glided into the fog and spiralled through the clouds to land by the constraints around _465_'s feet.

"Stop! no further! A muted voice commanded in the background, and in the road loomed a massive gate that slammed shut driven by the agressive breath of the Master."

Mr. Foster shivered, unprepared, as he viewed the drama in action before him. Sensitively, the butterfly's gentle mouth pulled at the fetters.

The tense figure of _465_ opened his eyes, puzzled, as he experienced the unfamiliar touch of sensitivity and care for his well being.

_465_ looked down at Truth, the butterfly, pulling at the shackles around his feet. The fluttering sound travelled through the air in front of his eyes. As he moved his head the muscles cracked and the neck brace opened as if unlocked by a key. He blinked repeatedly in rhythm with the butterfly's wings and stared at the shackles around his bleeding ankles.

As the butterfly flew down and tugged at the knotted cords again, freedom dawned. The figure was replaced by an eight legged wonder. Mr. Foster saw Ananse raise his head proudly when he realised that the cords were not shackles, they were pieces of his web.

Ananse looked puzzled over who had held his mind and restricted his movements into the future. The twisted tendrils he felt constricting his limbs were the threads of the web spun by the spider and his forefathers, revealing wisdom and creativity amongst the complexities of life.

They were the structure of a rich history, like contours of a high mountain which he could climb and from where he could view the world at his feet. The mountain with endless rivers was leading to new lands and limitless horizons.

"Tiger, wah gowaan? Yuh a try fi tief mi story dem agen?" Ananse questioned.

Mr. Foster continued to watch the drama roll out before him across continents and histories. He gasped as Ananse pulled himself with renewed vigour over the numerous contours from the centre of the web, changing from a spider into a man as it suited the occasion.

22

"The twisted tendrils he thought were constraining his limbs were the threads of the web spun by the spider and his forefathers revealing wisdom and creativity amongst the complexities of life."

Ananse's multitudinous eyes stared undaunted. He stretched his vision far into the horizon carrying Mr. Foster with him.

A deep fog arose in the outline of an old slave ship. It swept around Ananse trying to capture him once more. He used the gaining strength in his lengthy limbs to pull back the misery and agony of the memories in the ship's hold. Ananse moved on and the fog cleared.

 GYE NYAME: Except for God

Supremacy of God

The shape of a familiar continent he felt he had not seen since childhood came into view. Africa loomed like an estranged Mother, holding out her arms. Ananse ran into the open limbs and found himself looking out of the branches of a shade tree. It was evening time, and underneath the tree a lady was pointing towards him whilst telling stories to a group of children sitting at her feet.

"The web in which Kwaku Ananse lives, reaches from our earth to the Heavens, where Nyame the Sky God looks down with care for His creatures. Ananse is the messenger spreading wisdom to us all through his stories," she explained.

Motherland

Ananse's eyes opened wider and he looked beyond the mountain top and the widening oceans, to the revealed Motherland of Africa. He saw the web contours stretching to the ultimate land in the heavens that he remembered was also his home.

An empowered new figure emerged as the stories about him, told across the years, came back like a refreshing stream. He listened in amazement as the story teller continued.

The memories invigorated the suppressed energy in his mind and limbs. The same tales that had travelled from Africa, through the misery of the slave ships to the new lands of the Caribbean and the Americas, redefined themselves in the experiences of the unwilling travellers and their descendants. Memories of how he changed form in the tales to meet the new challenges, and Tiger taking on the role of the oppressor, came flooding back.

Ananse picked up his bright Kente cloth shirt and draped it around his shoulders. He proudly remembered that the inspiration for the pattern weaved in the cloth, as legend says, came from observations of his forefathers weaving their webs.

More than slavery

Once more Mr. Foster saw the outline figure of ~~465~~ rise up in the background. But this time he watched the figure take out his pen and cross through the three numbers etched in his mind, ~~465~~. Mr. Foster felt he was there as well helping to hold the pen. He was sharing the same thoughts as Truth, revealing the fact that his history was more than slavery. That had been merely a blot on the horizon in the building of the web that stretched across the earth to the heavens. His humanity had always been there under the criminal numerals of deception.

He looked further at the three numbers that had been written and realised that the handwriting was that of the many masters who had tried to conquer his people and his mind before emancipation. Were these the ones whose footsteps he was still subconsciously following in obedience today?

Real emancipation, he thought, was not on the paper many years ago but in his own mind today. That legal freedom had yet to be transformed into reality for many. For some the experiences of slavery are still within living memory. With the bondage of imposed inferiority of race and social position, they still linger on within societies across the oceans today. This has lead to an atmosphere of powerlessness and dependency in many places. Some even feel they were branded with the names forced upon them and passed down to the new generations.

The numbers disappeared from the page and Mr. Foster watched Ananse rise up with a new found vigour.

The creative creature reached over and pulled a piece of bark off a tree. He dropped it into a pot with some iron to make a dye. As the iron fell he envisaged the shackles in his mind melting into the boiling liquid. Picking up a calabash he carved the powerful new thoughts into symbolic shapes to pass on the messages running like wildfire through his brain.*   *Adinkra - Akan symbols

With renewed vigour he stamped the images onto cloth ready to send. He spoke out loudly, "Mi wanda who a go need dis?"

Mr. Foster heard his voice and immediately thought about his grand children. "Ananse, you'll soon have a new job to do. Get ready!" he said. Following this experience, he stood once more, confidently, with his family at the Golden Gates.

NKYIN KYIN: Twistings
Versatility, initiative, dynamism

The yellow butterfly, Truth, was perched beside Ananse and watched in amazement as he slowly twisted himself around, hiding behind the branches on the tree. The figure creatively shed his skin like a change of clothes and the spider figure reappeared. Ananse smiled the biggest smile that had ever crossed his lips.

The butterfly turned to him and said, "Ananse, others need to experience what you just went through."

"Look pon yuh now! Some people tink yuh just a ginnal,* but me know betta, yuh more dan dat!" He laughed knowingly, and winked at Ananse.

*Ginnal - trickster, using wit to outsmart others.

"Come with me and we'll follow the web trail to find the stories of those that fought against their plight in slavery. You won't find many of them in the books of the former slave masters. We need to remember that History isn't one story but many stories. We must find them for real freedom. Den we hav fi find a way fi pass dem on! "

"We must not forget the atrocities of slavery. But now we should learn from them and celebrate the contribution of the real heroes to the journey along the road to full freedom that we should all be aiming for."

The butterfly continued, "Mi ave a whole heap o sinting fi do. Will you help me Anansi?" He smiled.

"Weh yuh seh? Of course I will," Ananse laughed. "As you said, mi nah jus a ginnal, at least not all the time! I am clever. I was originally sent down to this world to spread wisdom and I will still do that job, even if it takes my ginnal character to do it! How do you think my stories survived for all these years? And, we must fly to the feet of the children of the slave masters themselves, and others living in the old master's lands, for many of them also need freedom."

"Lies and deceit have trapped them. Many think that Africa and her children are an uncivilised hindrance. Social control by the choice few is often seen as the only way to move forward. Mi know more dan dem bout de real Africa!"

"I know you do," said Truth. "But there is little acceptance that the continent of Africa, and the lands of the old plantations, are still suffering from this dire exploitation. European countries continue to build on the economic foundation laid during that time. Little responsibility is taken for the present day remnants of the actions of their forefathers, and divide and rule tactics are allowed to shrewdly continue."

"Now we have different forms of racism that are subtly as binding as the shackles that you, Ananse, thought were around your ankles and neck in the drama we were just watching. Real freedom is the right of every man not a reward for good works or a gift from a charity."

Truth fluttered his colourful wings and Ananse watched as he glided off through the archives picking the dots off the i's and the crosses off the t's trying to reach the central heart of humanity. Ananse followed, trying to keep up with him, swinging expertly across his web like a gymnast.

On the way they saw a closed gate on the edge of a playground. They both rested there for a while thinking of the children they could see in front of them and the new energy they could invigorate to impact on sustainable progress. 'Unite and make a difference' is the answer, not 'Divide and rule.'

What has happened to Martin Luther King's

dream? Have many, across the old triangle forgotten his plea and retreated into a nightmare?

Truth spread his wings and flew over the gate into the playground.

SHACKLES AND WEBS

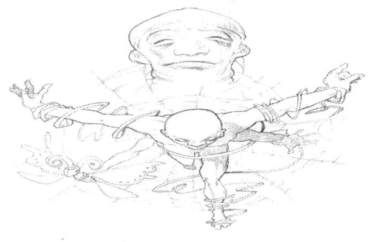

The twisted tendrils he thought were constraining his limbs were the threads of the web spun by the spider and his forefathers revealing wisdom and creativity amongst the complexities of life.

PART TWO

At their feet

A group of pupils had just finished listening to a story about Ananse and Tiger in their English lesson. The focus had been on traditional tales. The bell rang for break time so they went outside and began playing football with the others.

32

Soon a ball bounced over by the gate on the edge of the yard that led into an open space. The gate was closed during school time with an iron chain. As John bent down to pick up the ball, with Jason following him, a butterfly flew down and landed on the chain moving his wings slowly up and down in front of them.

Subconsciously following the butterfly's leading they saw that stretched between the chain and the gate was a spider's web. As they leaned over, Ananse peered down at them from a nearby branch and smiled.

John looked up and saw him. "Ananse!" he gasped, "I was just listening to some of your stories. Why haven't I heard them before? Tell me more. There is so much I don't understand."

"Some of the things I am hearing in the classroom and in the news don't make sense. Last week in my history lesson I asked my teacher some questions and he got angry with me and called my mom."

John continued, "You came from Africa, how? What's this slave thing? There is no way people just sat down and took it. Why don't we hear more about the heroes?
What about Africa?
What really happened there,
and in the Caribbean
and America? And who
is Tiger?"

33

"Wat a whole heap o question!" said Ananse. He smiled a huge spider smile and began talking enthusiastically. The dialogue continued.

Tendai, Aisha and Abenaa saw them together and came over to see what was happening. They stared in amazement at the talking spider. Ananse was telling incredible stories of ancient civilisations, discoveries, uprisings and inventions that opened their minds.

"You can do more than survive," said Ananse. "If you ever knew the things I've been through. Did you know that nobody wanted me to have what are now called Ananse stories?"

"Check out my encounter with Tiger, mek mi tell yuh bout him."

"Tiger was very selfish. Once, it seemed as if everything in the forest had Tiger's name, including all the stories. Im neva did wan fi talk to mi den. Tiger tried to trick me and I did what he didn't expect me to do. All the animals were amazed when I outsmarted him. Now the stories have my name!"

"This is how it started," he said, as he jumped enthusiastically onto his web. Everyone moved closer. "It was nightfall and the shadows were beginning to gather," he continued.

"Crick!" said Ananse. "Bring the story alive."

"Crack!" the young people replied.*

*Opening the story, bringing the spirit of the story alive.

"It was one of those days," Ananse continued, "when Tiger was showing off, big time! I met him under a huge tree and he didn't even look at me when I called to him. I was feeling rather fed up, but still a likkle facety.* 'Tiger,' I said, 'you have so many things called by your name, like Tiger Lilies and Tiger Moths, and the stories that everyone listens to as the sun goes down in the evening when we are all relaxed after a busy day. You know the ones I mean?' "   * a bit cheeky

"Tiger just growled and didn't even cast his eyes my way. 'Please, King Tiger, mek mi ave jus one o dem story wid mi name! Mi nuh ave nuttin!' "

"At that point I realised that other animals had gathered around. Tiger turned and looked straight in my eyes, opened his mouth and roared. Then he raised his head and laughed so loud that the trees shook and the other animals trembled as if rocked by the vibrations of his voice."

"There was a break in the laughter and Tiger looked at me once more with a sly grin on his face. 'Ananse,' he said, 'OK, yuh can ave dem. Yeh, ALL o dem!' I stared at him and so did all the other animals. Then he continued, 'If, Ananse, yuh ketch Missa Snake fi mi. Yuh know de long, long, fat sinting dat live down by de riva? Den yuh can ave ALL o de story dem!' "

"At that point he started laughing again, and all the animals joined in and stared at me."

"So how did you do it?" John asked him.

"Well," Ananse continued, "The idea didn't come to me straight away. I went down by the river, hid in the grass and just looked at Mr. Snake. He was so, so, so long! I thought there was no chance I would be able to catch him, and I was going to look like a fool!"

"He didn't see me, and I did the first thing I could think of. With all my strength I dug a pit and threw in some of snake's favourite fruit. Then I found some greasy, coconut sinting* and put it around the side. I waited a while and snake smelt the fruit. He almost slid down the hole but soon noticed the grease and realised he wouldn't be able to get out again."   *something greasy from the coconut

"Did he find a way?" James asked,

"I didn't think he would, but he managed to twist himself around a tree and reach for the fruit without slipping down."

"I tried a few more tricks, but I could see he was getting suspicious. Then I noticed some bamboo was growing close by and one of the longest pieces had broken off and fallen down. He was even longer than that! That's when the idea came to me."

"Come on," Aisha gasped, "What did you do?"

Anansi chuckled, "You are not going to believe snake was so stupid. He called to me and said, 'Anansi, some strange tings a gowaan, yuh a try fi trick mi?' "

"I looked at him and said, 'Nah Missa snake, mi jus try fi mek a point. Snake, yuh so, so, so long; mi

36

neva know dat. Mi jus lef de odder animal dem, an Tiger. Dem jus a chat a whole heap o foolishness bout yuh. Dem say dat yuh nat de longis creature inna de fores!' "

"Snake turned his eyes towards me and said, 'Wah? Anansi, mi kyaan be boddered wi dis, of course mi a de longis. Look pon dat piece o bamboo over deh so, mi longa dan dat!' "

" 'Mi know dat!' I replied. 'Mek mi bring it ova an lay it beside yuh fi prove it.' It wasn't very easy for me, but I managed to drag it closer to snake and he wriggled beside it."

" 'Wait Missa Snake,' I said carefully. 'One problem, de animal dem soon com fi see wah gowaan, an we ave fi get it right. If mi go one end o de bamboo fi see weh yuh tail is, an den go down de odder end fi look weh yuh head is, an yuh nat really dat long, yuh might try fi slidda down an trick mi.' "

" 'Ananse, yuh tink mi woulda do dat?' he answered. 'OK,' he continued, 'Mek mi tell yuh. Tek a piece o dat wis* over deh an tie mi tail to de bamboo so mi kyaan move. Den mi can stretch an stretch an yuh can tie mi neck as well. Call dem creatures, especially boasy Tiger an mek we show dem!' "   *withes, creepers.

"So that's what I did," Ananse stated. The group around him opened their mouths in amazement.

"Then I ran faster than I've ever run before on

37

my eight legs. 'Tiger, kom! Mi ketch Missa Snake!' I shouted through the trees."

"Every creature in the forest followed Tiger that day. When he saw Snake, and knew that everyone had heard what he had said to me, that was it! From that time onwards all the stories in the forest became called Ananse stories. Mine!"

"Jackmandora," Ananse said.

"Mi nuh choose none," the group stated.*

*Story ending: Disclaimer - 'I told the story but I'm not responsible for the content.'

"Yes, the stories are called Ananse stories now, but they are not just for me. They are for all the animals in the forest, and for you too! Later on the bees in the trees thought I was trying to catch them too, because of another one of Tiger's tricks. But what I really wanted was for them to fly around and take the stories for everyone to hear."

He twisted all his hairy legs like an acrobat and span around the dangling web. "Look pon mi nuh! You see this web? I can go anywhere on this, all over the world and even into the heavens. Mi nah jus a ginnal, mi clever!"

"But, I'll have to watch. I think Tiger was trying to trap me and get the stories back again just now. He had a go at the same kind of tricks. He took me back in time to when my stories travelled in people's minds on the slave ships while crossing the oceans from Africa to the Caribbean and American lands. He was trying to make me feel that I was in chains and worth nothing. But his plan didn't work, because, little did he know, it wasn't really him in control! He twisted the story and hid the fact that it was creative tactics like mine that helped the enslaved people to survive, and eventually get their freedom!"

"Wow!" John exclaimed. "I think we have a similar job to do. It seems that the stories about our history in Africa, the Caribbean, and other lands have been owned by a Tiger, not us; and not been told properly. In fact, I think Tiger only lets us have what he can keep control of, without us realising it."

"We are going to have to play smart like you to get the stories back. Then we can spread them round in our own way for everyone to hear, so we can manage our own lives."

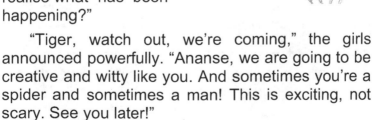

"John, you're right; and we are going to need all the bees to help us, just like in your stories Ananse, here, in Africa and the Caribbean," Jason joined in. "I wonder if people realise what has been happening?"

"Tiger, watch out, we're coming," the girls announced powerfully. "Ananse, we are going to be creative and witty like you. And sometimes you're a spider and sometimes a man! This is exciting, not scary. See you later!"

The bell rang. As the pupils headed towards the

school building Truth once again began to energise his wings and followed them.

The real story of Shackles and Webs

Back in the classroom John and Jason sat down in front of the computer and started to plan their next topic. The teacher had given them a free choice to name and design it themselves. 'Emancipation', they called it, 'The real story of Shackles and Webs.'

"John, look at this," Jason said enthusiastically as he searched new sites. "The only thing I was ever taught in school about my history was slavery, as told by the slave master; poverty in Africa and Carnival in Jamaica."

"Then I look at the TV and a lot of the people that look like me seem to be portrayed as gangsters, people in trouble, or people who have sold out their culture! That's Tiger's doing."

"There is so much to find out. Ananse has opened my eyes. We need to explore this history. I feel someone has been holding me back, making me feel ashamed, as if I'm not good enough, telling me what I should be. There is a whole web of knowledge just waiting for us out there."

They both looked back at the flickering screen and Ananse appeared before them sitting on his web on the edge of a Golden gate.

Truth once more fluttered through the fog carrying a key. He inserted it into the rusty lock around the gate post and turned it slowly to the right.

The

lock

burst open

and

fell

to the

ground.

The

Golden Gates

Opened

Before

Them

Numerous icons appeared before Jason and John. Ananse swung down from his web and clicked the mouse. One at a time the icons revealed the extent of the web.

"Thank you, Ananse. Look, Jason, at our family across the world."

Miss. Smith looked worried as she heard raised voices at John and Jason's desk. Their enthusiasm emanated beyond the computer screen in front of them. She got up ready to tell them to turn off the game programme she expected to see on the screen.

"Miss, look at this!"

A yellow butterfly looked over John and Jason's shoulders. He fluttered his wings and the teacher gazed in amazement, new thought streams pouring into her mind.

Jason's eyes were wide open as tales of ancient heroes, merchants, farmers, inventors, musicians, craft workers and discoverers flashed over the screen. With each click of the mouse Africa, the real Motherland, provided the backdrop to the scenes before him. This was followed by the new horizons of the Diaspora in the Caribbean, American and European lands where the inventiveness had continued, even under extreme oppression.

The river flows

Truth, the butterfly, picked up a paint brush and began coating the top corner of the screen as it appeared like a canvass. He created the source of a flowing river. With fast, energetic strokes the spring burst into the picture like a new born child.

The powerful rush of water broke through the hard terrain and a new valley was born. The paint brush strokes slowed down and the blue water settled into a rhythmic flow across the plains.

Miss watched the flow across the screen with a puzzled expression. Suddenly the lightening flashed and thunder cracked like an angry whip! The steady rhythm of the waves turned into a boiling cauldron battling against the force of the storm. She saw a desperate figure struggling along the path at the side of the river.

The thunder cracked again and the ensuing rain moved parts of the river onto new paths not of its choosing. The steep banks restricted the direction of the flow and, as the force of the storm subsided, the rhythm of the river settled back into a regular flow in its new lands.

The butterfly was having problems with the brush at this stage and did not seem to know where to direct the strokes on the canvass. He flew onto the edge of the screen and put the brush back into the paint pot. The gates closed once more.

John and Jason became unsettled while this was going on....*465 465 465 465*....flashed across the screen.

The boys blinked their eyes and shook their heads in confusion, unable to define strange thoughts going through their minds.

They pushed Ananse out of the way and clicked onto a smiling icon at the side of the screen. In a short while they were distracted onto a new game and giggles began. Tendai and Abenaa came and sat beside them.

"Can we play too?" they asked.

"What? You don't know about computers; you wouldn't know what to do!" Jason said sarcastically.

John joined in the laughter and a tear fell from Tendai's eye as she said, "What are you talking about? You are the uncivilized ones. You don't have any history anyway, no names of your own, and no language of your own!"

Aisha heard the conversation and looked over, gasping as John reached out his hand to strike out at Tendai. He knocked Jason instead and the chair almost tipped over.

"Get off, leave me alone!" Jason retaliated angrily. He pushed John and he fell to the floor.

"Stop, you lot and get on with your work, or I'll keep you behind." Miss raised her voice. "I knew you were up to no good, you are all the same." She had quickly forgotten about the canvass and the new thought streams went from her mind...*465*... *465*... *465*... drifted by.

SANKOFA: **Return and get it**
Learn from the past

Ananse knew that his job was not over. The old river needed rejuvenating or images of the past would continue to take over in a negative way. After renewal, the blue print can then be used to determine the path into the future. He picked up the brush and placed it carefully back into Truth's hand. He smiled a knowing smile.

From above, a flutter was heard and a new shape flew into the picture. The Akan, Sankofa bird landed near by and began walking alongside, leading Truth with the brush, back to the source of the river. There he helped him to retrace the journey of the flow.

Overlooking the water, the creative tendrils of Ananse's web made a pattern in the sky. From his web Ananse reached over and touched Miss's hand. She turned her head and stared at him. Ananse whispered to her, "No, Miss, don't give up, watch what is happening." Then he seemed to disappear.

She looked back at the canvass as Truth was fluttering over the spring. The humming sound took on a rhythm and John and Jason turned around.

Through the stream of water they could see the shadow of a prosperous continent. The web images the boys were looking at earlier came back to life. All now deeply interested they continued to follow the flow of the river.

Unnoticed before were Truth and Ananse sailing on a boat across the waves with the Sankofa bird flying above. They pointed to the landscapes on the banks of the river and saw again the heroes and inventors in the ancient African lands.

Rough waves started to rise and the storm began again. Ananse's boat stayed its ground and alongside his vessel other vessels became visible. As the audience looked on, the lightening flashed and the intensity of the storm grew stronger.

But with each crash the crews rowed in harmony creating a new rhythm to battle through the storm. They had little choice of direction but overcoming the obstacles gave them fresh strength and new heroes arose.

The spectators were beginning to view the canvass in a new light but it didn't stop there. With each flash of lightening they realised there was more than one artist. The Master of the lightening flashes was trying to control, but his ambition was selfish.

The vessels struggled through the storm and the river settled in the new lands. As the storm subsided, the crews looked for strength and guidance to help them decide what routes to take into the future.

SHACKLES AND WEBS

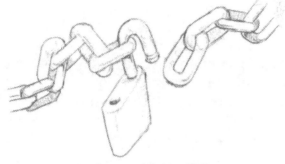

PART THREE

Freedom

"**G**ood morning everyone! Today we are going to share with you…..**Emancipation: the REAL story of Shackles and Webs.**" Jason and John spoke boldly, as they stood up in assembly, with Tendai, Aisha and Abenaa, to give their presentation to the school, parents and other guests.

Miss watched proudly from her seat at the side of the hall. She had realised that the journey travelled by the young people over the last few weeks, in the preparation of their topic, was an experience that had to be shared.

It was the first time they had played such a role. As they looked at their parents, with a new found confidence, their voices rang out across the room.

"This is not going to be a usual assembly. It will be more like a conversation. We are going to talk to you about our experiences during the journey we just travelled," John explained.

"We are beginning to understand how to make sense of history," said Jason. "It is like following a river. We have to look at where it's coming from and what is happening at the time that affects its flow. There may be rocky places, storms and lightening flashes, or valleys and quiet places. And it depends on who is telling the story and where they are positioned while looking at the scene."

"Yes," John carried on, "this has helped us to work out how to deal with having slavery in our history. I thought it was just about shackles, and I didn't really want to know. But it's much more than that, and the legacy of slavery is in ALL our histories in some form."

He raised his hand and moved it across the hall passing everyone in its path.

"Now listen to 'OURstories!' "

FAWODHODIE ENE OBRE NA NAM:

Independence comes with its responsibilities.

Independence, freedom, emancipation

"We ALL need to learn what is real Emancipation and Freedom. And Tiger! This time WE are telling the story with Ananse and the bees beside us!" As he spoke Jason wriggled his hands like a spider. John growled deeply like a Tiger and the girls buzzed like bees in the background.

He continued boldly, "Ananse has opened our eyes. There is a whole web of knowledge just waiting for us out there. We have put a display on the wall outside about Ananse, when he thought he had nothing and Tiger had everything."

"No, we are not crazy, his stories came from Africa and travelled across the world in the minds of our ancestors, that's why he understands what we are trying to say today! Africa is a massive continent," continued John. "It was the cradle of human civilization, connecting all of us in eras of inventiveness and purpose, way before the transatlantic trade. Tendai and Abenaa have been telling us some old, old stories. Tendai speaks Shona, and Abenaa speaks Twi, those are African languages."

"Yes," Abenaa continued, "I have been trying to understand many of these things as well, to work out what went wrong. Transatlantic slavery was selfish and unfair and the legacy continues long after the trade was supposed to have been abolished. Sadly, forms of slavery are still happening in our world today."

"During the period we are talking about many were guilty. People were tricked, used and hurt, and some were forced into actions against their own people. Thousands, maybe millions, died along the journeys and on the plantations."

"It was a time when different worlds were trying to link and trade. Many mistakes were made because the focus was self centred. The routes across the oceans formed the shape of a triangle from Europe to Africa, to the New Worlds and then back to Europe. Goods were exchanged for people, and then people were used for labour to produce more goods to be sent back to the European lands. But the people used were enslaved, denied their humanity and manipulated as tools to profit others. It was the largest, twisted, world enterprise and the worst transgression ever against humanity!"

Abenna shook her head in disbelief. "We are calling it the Transatlantic Maafa. Maafa is a Swahili word meaning disaster, terrible occurrence or great tragedy."

"But even during these dreadful times there were people from MY Africa, some of YOUR ancestors, who stood up for freedom and fairness. Many of them gave their lives in the process." Abenna continued, "There were countless uprisings and campaigns across the years by many of ALL our ancestors on the different sides of the trading triangle who knew that it was wrong. They continued until others started listening and change began to happen."

Aisha pointed to the display they had put together. Standing tall she spoke out confidently, "We're so proud of them! There are too many to number and many whose names we will never know. Here are some examples we have on our display."

"We MUST start by remembering first of all those who suffered and those who died in Africa on the way to the ships; on the Middle Passage across the oceans, and on the plantations, in dire conditions that we cannot possibly imagine! We will never know exactly how many, and there will never be enough time or enough words to say what needs to be said about them!" She sighed deeply.

"Next, we have examples of people in Africa who stood for freedom like Queen Nzinga Nbande, from Angola who formed an army against the Portuguese slave traders. King Affonso from Kongo was the first ruler to resist the European slave trade."

"There were also many uprisings, particularly in the Caribbean. And then there were former slaves, like Olaudah Equiano, who wrote about their experiences. He became a key spokesman in the anti slavery movement in England. These uprisings, and stories such as his, fueled a growing abolitionist movement influencing people like

51

William Wilberforce. But we don't hear enough about those stories!"

Aisha showed them further pictures on the display. "Here are Sam Sharpe and Paul Bogle who are now recognised as Jamaican National Heroes. I was proud to learn about them in school in Jamaica. Sam Sharpe led a Christmas rebellion in Jamaica and paid for it with his life. His words were, 'I'd rather die on yonder gallows than live the life of a slave.' As a deacon he used his Christian teaching to move ahead the anti slavery movement."

"People like Paul Bogle continued the cause years after slavery was supposed to have been abolished. He lead the Morant Bay Rebellion in Jamaica which made the Government listen to the needs of the people whose lives were still no better. He too died in the process. Then many others, like Alexander Bustamante, continued the ongoing fight for freedom from Colonial control."

"We must remember Haiti's role as well, in travelling the seas to capture slavers, and in looking after those who fled to its shorelines to escape slavery."

"There were also people like John Newton who was a Slave Trader. He eventually realized that he was in the middle of something that was wrong and changed the direction of his life to make a difference. He wrote the song 'Amazing Grace,' where he says he once was blind but now he can see; and he thanked God for saving a wretch like himself."

"Other key people like the Quakers drove the abolition movement forward. The struggle to end these wrong doings was long one. But it shouldn't have taken so long!" Aisha raised her voice confidently, "We have to follow NOW in the footsteps of those people who recognised the injustices and continue their stand today for freedom and fairness for all."

John stood beside Aisha and spoke boldly, "There is so much still to do across the Diaspora."

Tendai announced, "Now we are going to have two minute's silence to remember all these people. But first…"

John and Jason sat behind the drums and the sound began……

Brrumpumpum, Brrumpumpum,

Abenaa spoke up confidently, "Listen! In 1937 William Prescott, a former slave wrote….

'They will remember that we were sold,
But they won't remember that we were strong.
They will remember that we were bought,
But not that we were brave.' "

"Let us make him proud today!"

They all chanted in rhythm with the beat…

"Bow your heads and remember,
Lift them up and say thanks

To the
STRONG and the **BRAVE**,
To the many who suffered,
To the many who died,
To the many who stood
For Freedom, for Justice
Across the Atlantic
So now we can all be proud of who we are,
Have hope today,
And live and work equally together
In all the lands."

Silence came upon the congregation in the hall. All heads bowed as the seconds ticked by.

The minutes passed and Jason clapped his hands; everyone in front of him raised their heads and joined in with a cheer. ......

The drum beat rounded off the voices and each person in the hall stood tall!

Brrumpumpum, Brrumpumpum,

pum, pum, pum, pum.

WAWA ABA: Seed of the wawa tree
Persevere through hardship
Jason stated, "We must understand that stories during this time were full of resistance and rebellion. No, people did NOT just take what was done to them! They were very creative in finding ways to fight against the wrong things happening to them, and they even invented ways to talk to each other through codes in drum rhythms and songs.

Ananse, they used the same tactics to beat the Tigers who were in control as you did in your stories!"

"Another other thing that I didn't realise before," he continued with enthusiasm, "was that even out of wrong people made good things happen. Then others continued to build on that legacy afterwards."

"One of those things was....Music, like Spirituals and Jazz; but not just to entertain. People were able to spread messages through music when their voices were otherwise not listened to, both during slavery and other times of oppression. Even now we enjoy and gain strength from these music styles."

"Later on Reggae developed and Bob Marley arose as another one of those special people. We are still listening to his messages today. Through music he brought people together emphasising culture and strength in unity. As a Rastafarian he held on strongly to his African roots and his music was more powerful than politics."

"February has now been declared Reggae Month in Jamaica because of the powerful messages that he spread across the oceans."

"The Wailers sang, 'No chains about my feet, but I'm not free.' So Bob Marley said that something needed to happen, people must take responsibility for their Freedom so that their minds can focus on success." Jason turned on the CD player and the message was heard in the background....

'Emancipate yourselves from mental slavery;

None but ourselves can free our minds.'

"In fact we are using music in the same way, even now," he continued. "But we've got to make sure we get out the right messages. We need to build on the legacy of Reggae to pass on what we really need today."

"Listen! This is **our** message to other young people as they grow up in this world. There are a lot of negative pressures out there in society and on the streets that we must not follow. I think Tiger is in control of many of the lyrics we hear today so he can keep us apart and make some money for himself!"

"Let's use our talents and our voices for **Real Freedom**." The drums started….
Bbuchacha, bbuchacha, bbuchacha.

The beat continued in the background….
Bbuchacha, bbuchacha, cliick cliick,
Then Jason began….
"Things have changed,
Once some people were tied!
Bbuchacha, bbuchacha, cliick cliick,
Now no longer have chains,
No whips, no shackles,
Not even one cane.
No longer pushed down,
You're invincible,
Man!! It's your world. It's your world.
Bbuchacha, bbuchacha, cliick cliick,

It's not about the streets,
Spittin bars about fake beef.*
What you chattin bout,
Life's not about hurtin, chillin an buillin,**
It's all about livin.
Make your own choices,
It's your world, it's your world.
Don't just talk,
Make it happen,
Work as one,
Make a difference for the betta,
Live!! It's your world. It's your world."
Cliick cliick,cliick cliick,cliick cliick.

*Creating trouble about nothing, don't like the person or crew.
**life's not about hurting people, wasting time doing nothing,
drinking and taking drugs.

Abenaa pointed to the drums and stated, "Yes, we have to be careful that we use our music to work together to make a difference, not to divide and hurt others. Racism is out there, we need to fight it, not each other."

"There are some who would like to see that happen, then they can stay in control. That's an old way of misusing power that is still going on. We must be proud of who we are and be the best in everything we do."

"And there is food, like my Nan's sweet potato pudding and jerk chicken," Aisha stated, licking her lips. "New dishes were invented by creative people when dem a fe mek a way outta no way."

"There were people like the Maroons who

resisted slavery long before abolition. They have kept lots of the African traditions alive. They have their own language, 'Kromanti', and govern themselves even now. Grandy Nanny of the Maroons is one of the heroes I learned about in school in Jamaica. Abenaa has been telling us that Nanna means Chief in Ghana. These stories are not told enough, and in some places not at all. Change needs to take place!"

"Wait, there's my hero too, another woman, Mbuya Nehanda, from Zimbabwe." Tendai's voice rose enthusiastically, "She was strong and determined like Nanny, standing up for freedom in my country during a difficult time when others were trying to control. Mbuya means grandmother. She is known as the grandmother of Zimbabwe and her spirit of freedom also lives on. We need to preserve her legacy today."

"And, there's my hero too. I know you are still listening, Ananse!" James' voice was enthusiastic and he laughed. "In fact your stories are all over the place; you have webs in every corner. You are using those tales to teach lessons even more than the teachers. It was Ananse's web that helped me to see how far across the world and the heavens my heritage comes from. Ananse, you have plenty of work to do!"

"Sorry Miss, but the stories do work if you tell them right. Children have to listen, they can't help it!"

58

"Jason, you carry on," Miss spoke up. "I have been listening to him as well."

"Really, Miss!" said Jason in astonishment. He continued, "And some other things that work are games where you have to use strategies to stretch your mind."

"Yes," joined in Tendai, "I know you use some of the same ones we have in Africa that travelled to the lands we have talked about. My favourite one is Wari and playing it made me like maths."

"I'll have to try that one; we could set up an after school club to learn how to play the game," suggested Jason. "This is all so unbelievable. And we have to recognise that strong, new, creative cultures have developed, and are still developing, across the Caribbean and American lands. These have now spread wherever people have travelled since these times. And I am here now!"

"New languages formed as people who spoke different languages had to communicate with each other. And guess what; Jamaican is being more recognised as a language now!"

"Many of us while we were growing up were told not to speak like that, speak proper English. Now they are realising that Jamaican is a language we can be proud of. It has developed in the same way that other languages across the world have developed."

John stood up straight and put his hands like a tree, "A weh yuh seh? Cooyah!" he continued. "A fi mi langwij!* People without knowledge of their past history, origin and culture are like a tree without roots."

"Yes," Aisha joined in, "Marcus Garvey said that. He was another one of the Jamaican heroes and Africa was very special to him too."

*"What did you say? Listen here!........ This is my language!"

 AYA FERN: Fern
Endurance and resourcefulness.
"New inventors and scientists arose," Jason carried on, "like Garrett Morgan, Louis Latimer and Charles Drew in America; and Richard Hill, Dr. Lecky and Professor Louis Grant in Jamaica. Then there were those who stood against unfairness like the pioneer nurse Mary Seacole."

"New governments have formed. New leaders arose like Marcus Garvey, who stood for Justice and Equality. He said that we must learn our real history in school and he told people who acted like Tiger to keep away and let us have Real Freedom."

"Institutes and councils were set up in Jamaica to encourage more research, find uses for the country's own resources and to encourage Literature, Science and the Arts, to move people forward to our New Futures. One of my uncles told me this; he is in Kingston, Jamaica, at the University."

Now there are key black leaders in the governments across the Atlantic. In our town there are new preachers like my Uncle Sam, and new businesses like my Mom and Dad's, and - **ME!**"

"This does not excuse the wrong, but it makes me realise I must never give up aiming for my goals. We need to be agents of change not the victims." Jason grew in stature as he spoke, "We are born to be great!"

"Do you know what the last four letters of Jamaican and African are?" The young people said together.....

"I CAN!"

They continued.....

"Sometimes I feel like
I must be running a race.
I need encouragement,
Tell me I can, not I can't
The track is long and
The cheers of the crowd encourage me,
So don't try to discourage me,
Tell me I can, not I can't."

The crowd in the hall clapped and Jason and John's parents stood in support of their sons. Aisha's Aunty stood as well, proud that her sister in Jamaica had given her the chance to support her daughter's schooling. Circumstances had been very difficult in the area she was from but some inner strength had kept them going. They all thought of the grand parents who had paved the way on both sides of the oceans, and had diligently strived to overcome the closure of the gates blocking their vision for the future.

Abenaa and Tendai's parents joined them remembering the ancient histories of Africa that had formed the foundation for these new lands.

Jason continued, "As for names, Tendai and Abenaa, I do like the African ones. I might use some of them for my children, or invent my own. But even over the years we've taken the surnames that were given to us in the past and transformed the legacy in our families into something new and refreshing."

"Grandpa and Grandma Foster, we are proud of the name you have passed on to us, it's full of your hard work and determination. We wish you were here in the hall today."

"We are not finished yet!" John spoke out enthusiastically. "We must do all we can to make sure things like this do not happen again in our communities. We are all equal. We have to work together, encourage each other, and everyone here should have goals to aim for."

"If we know and are proud of who we are we feel strong. If we are confused about who we are we will feel lonely, mixed up and angry, and we will not achieve."

"We need to walk tall, not just dress good and show off. It's not what you have, it's who you are!"

John's voice resonated across the hall.

The young people stood together in a line and walked, heads held high, towards the audience. They turned together and made a circle, holding their hands up in the air.

DONO NTOASO: The double drum
Co-operation, agreement, and unity.
Tendai announced, "In Shona, working together is 'Kushanda tese,' and the Adinkra symbol 'Dono Ntoaso' means co-operation, agreement and unity. We are different, but we should unite. And I have learned that there is a Jamaican proverb that says, 'One han kyaan clap,' so that means we need all hands!"

"My American cousin," John said, "likes KWANZAA. That is a festival that is celebrated by African American families when they are together around Christmas and the New Year. There is a special word they use that means unity; UMOJA, it's a Swahili word."

"**TEAM - T**ogether **E**ach **A**chieves **M**ore."

"Miss, there is also an African proverb we can follow when we think about working together - 'It takes a whole village to raise a child.' "

Miss smiled and nodded her head powerfully in agreement. John said with confidence, "ME, I'm going to be a preacher and a lawyer so I can help others. Not just someone who can preach good sermons, but someone who helps people to grow, develop their skills, realise their responsibilities, get over obstacles and go out to make a difference."

"There is a lot of unfairness, poverty and crime out there. I want to help people work together, speak out for justice and make the right choices from their hearts. They must realise that it won't help to hurt each other or chase after material things before the things that really matter."

Aisha stepped forward, "I will join you, John. I want to be a scientist. Like you said, not someone that just talks, but someone who uses their knowledge to solve problems, build our Nations, and make the world a better place. Then dreams can be fulfilled!"

"Me, I'd like to be Ananse," Jason exclaimed, standing tall and waving his hands. "I've learned a lot from him. Stop laughing! You too Ananse! But I will make sure I always use your tactics for good! I'm going to design web sites where people can learn about history and science that will help them! SEE! And, I will spread the messages, Aisha and John, that you want me to send on my world wide web."

Yes!

Hold on," Tendai jumped in, "I'm going to be a teacher. And, I'm going to travel, to Africa, America and the Caribbean and make sure children learn their history and appreciate others."

"And me," said Abenaa, "I'm interested in all of this. I'm going to study history and find the real stories and the real heroes. Tiger watch it; they're not yours any more! Then I'll write a book to share across the Atlantic. Tendai, you can make sure the teachers use it in schools!"

"Now," exclaimed Jason, "I have a poem. To all parents, teachers and leaders! This is the difference that the message we have put over today can make to the lives of children and young people in our communities and in our schools."

He stood confidently, looking at the adults in the hall and spoke out.....

"CONNECTED

I saw a child with
Passive lips,
A lowered head,
Dark eyes staring
Into an unknown tomorrow.
I heard a sarcastic remark
Behind a glowing stare,
Masking a sunken spirit
Disconnected from education
By a bottomless abyss.

But…

He saw himself in history today.
For the first time his teacher's eyes met his,
Alive as he understood his yesterday
And hoped for his tomorrow.
He felt part of the school today.
His opinion was requested and his voice
Listened to.
He heard his voice in literacy today
'I am bilingual,
My language has a value like yours and
I have a history to be proud of,'

'**My story**.'

* Dai liat a sho tru de key hol
An fi im min' cum alif.
Im lips wan tase de sabby,
Nyam til im belly full.
Gi im di golen kie
An mek im burs inna de worl
Wid an enterprising spirit…
which says
I am
I can
I will !"

"A redi yuh redi aredi?
A kom mi kom fi kom wiet fi yuh!"

*Day light is showing through the key hole and his mind has come alive. His lips want to taste the knowledge, eat until he is full. Give him the golden key and let him burst into the world with…..
**Are you ready? I'm waiting for you.

66

"A redi, yuh redi aredi? Are you ready?" They all joined in and stood together holding their hands up high above their heads.

"Now we have a dance for you," Aisha stated. They stepped forward and in front of them were some stone shapes drawn on the ground.

"We are going to cross a muddy river and we don't want to get wet." The music started and they swayed from stone to stone carefully crossing the dangerous river.

"Bruckins," Aisha continued, "We're celebrating Emancipation like I did in Jamaica. By unfolding the story; one step at a time we'll get across the river. August 1st was set aside in Jamaica to celebrate Emancipation, and a special park was created in the centre of Kingston. It is full of trees and flowers and clear running water. People go there at all times of the day and late evening to walk, jog and enjoy their freedom. Lots of creative events are held there. It's called Emancipation Park."

As she spoke, Jason moved over to the drum set in the corner and began to play the rhythm to accompany the Spiritual they had chosen for the end of the assembly....

Bburummprummprumm,   Bburummprummprumm,

"Take the shackles off my feet so I can dance,
I just want to praise you,
I just want to praise you,
You broke the chains, now I can lift my hands,
And I'm gonna praise you,

67

I'm gonna praise you."

Bburummprummprumm,   Bburummprummprumm,

The beat of the drum quietened down into the background.....*Bburummprummprumm*

They spoke together confidently…

"We must remember,

We need to work together

Like these drums are doing,

Be strong in our mission,

Tune ourselves,

Make our own confident sound.

Then talk to the other drums,

Work creatively in harmony.

If we don't do this it will result

In discord and disaster."

"While we were planning this assembly," Tendai spoke up, "we had to learn a lot from each other and our families and put the pieces together ourselves. So many different stories! "

"James and John were born here in England. Their grandparents came from Jamaica, before Jamaica became independent, and they have relatives in America. Aisha was born in Jamaica and only came here two years ago. Abenaa is from Ghana and came here last year as I did from Zimbabwe. What an experience this has been!"

"Yes, it has, and I want to find out more," said John.

He continued, "Now, as you go out of the hall today you will be given a small badge to put on your jackets like the poppy that people wear to remember those who died in the world wars."

"This badge has on it the shape of the Sankofa bird to remind us to look back and remember those things we have talked about. All those who suffered and died, and those who fought for the freedom we have today."

"But it doesn't stop there, it also tells us to learn from them and go forward to make a difference in our world. Behind the bird there's an arrow with a new equilateral shape for us to build together."

"Let us pray before we leave." Aisha bowed her head.

"Dear God, thank you for all the things we have learned today. Help us to remember, learn from them and move forward. Give us the strength to work together and make a difference in our world today. Speak to those who need to make changes in their thinking to help repair the damages from the past. Amen."

The volume of the drums began to rise again as John played with growing enthusiasm.

Bburummprummprumm,   *Bburummprummprumm,*

Jason raised his voice and said, "Let's go! The world is waiting!"

As the pupils began streaming out of the hall the music in the background began playing…

'Open the flood gates of heaven,
Let it rain, let it rain.
Everybody needs some rain,
Let's feel the rain.
Everybody in this place feel the rain.
Maybe you need to look at
Somebody and tell them,
No more drought, it's raining,
Let the plants blossom and the flowers grow.'

Suddenly, there was a knock on the school hall door and the caretaker came in with a parcel. Everyone stopped to find out what was going on.

"Excuse me," he said. "This package just arrived for Jason, John, Aisha, Abenaa and Tendai. I can't read who it's from as there is a piece of spider web blocking the writing, and I don't want to touch it."

Aisha took the parcel and brushed off the web. "It just says – 'Dis a fi yuh. From Ananse'," she read as she opened the parcel.

Inside was a large piece of material with various symbols stamped on it.

"Come on," she continued, "let's find out what this is all about, I think Ananse is trying to send us

70

some messages."

They went out of the hall excited as they began to look at the Adinkra symbols Ananse had sent to them.

BOA ME NA ME MMOA WO: Help me and let me help you

Cooperation, interdependence

The lights burned late that night as Miss looked closely at the school curriculum. Truth the butterfly sat on her shoulder. As Miss read through the documents, she realised that the material had been sewn consistently with a biased thread. It was not easy for her. Although legal freedom was in place, she felt her own road, and that of many people in education, was already laid. It was constructed within a framework of ignorance, and worked with tools of racism, stereotypes and low expectations.

The pupils had inspired her. She began to see beyond the angry, puzzled faces of some she had taught, and acknowledged that it was not just the content of the lessons that needed to change but the expectations of the adults. They must give the children and young people a chance to learn about and value their heritage; be confident and creative, developing their skills and talents to prepare them for the world of the future.

Her concern was that she would have opposition from others who might feel they have an interest to protect. They must all understand....

"Freedom for one should mean Freedom for all." She found herself speaking out loud, thinking about how she was going to do this and teach about slavery and freedom so all would understand. She realised that all staff with a role in the education and social systems needed to be a part of this. She wondered if this was the same story in other schools across the oceans.

Looking down once again at the curriculum documents she saw the shadow of Ananse at the top of the page. He was holding a needle into which he was inserting a new piece of thread. He handed the needle to Miss telling her to pull hard and start sewing again.

As she drew the thread tightly through the fibres a change began to happen. It seemed as if the very movement away from the prejudicial weave of the old thread within the material was creating a mighty new order. This must be how Ananse planned his stories so that the powerless could become the powerful.

Miss herself felt stronger and more confident. She looked up at the window where a group of bees were buzzing around in a circle as if they were dancing.

NEA ONNIM NO SUA A, OHU: He who does not know can know from learning

Life-long education and continued quest for knowledge

As the parents and other visitors left the hall they were talking enthusiastically about their experiences.

Ananse looked down from his web in the rafters and beckoned to Truth, who was sitting on a strand of the web in the corner. "Tek dis nuh!" he said to the butterfly, and passed the reserve materials for further web design to Truth. Truth flew around threading the fibres in and out of the experiences drifting through the air.

Conversations became empowered as the various experiences linked and the web grew stronger and wider. New ideas flew creatively through the air, focussed on joint working, to support children in knowing and valuing their history and helping them to plan for the future. Then ideas came up around how they could feed this into the local schools and work together in partnership.

Some of them felt that often they had not been allowed to make their own choices and systems had restrained them with the same negative and manipulative tools. The result was that perhaps they had not tried to explore the rich histories in depth.

The parents were proud of their children's

vision, 'Together we can achieve more.' They felt a releasing of the invisible cords as plans unfolded. They looked down at their hands and saw that they were confidently gripping new tools to build the inventive framework that was being drawn up in their minds.

When Jason's mom reached home she picked up the phone.

"Momma, can we talk? John and Jason have opened up my mind today. You should have heard them in their assembly presentation this morning! Please, I want to know more about your experiences in Jamaica and coming to England. You all contributed so much. I know it wasn't easy for you. Your generation had to really stand up for your rights and set up many of the institutions that we take for granted today. You were the pioneers we must not forget."

"Shirley, thank you so much, I know you understand," Mrs. Foster answered. "What I am concerned about is preserving that heritage. We need more of our own galleries and museums. If we can put our experiences together, the sky's the limit. Or as we say in Jamaica – one, one coco full basket."

"Listen, wait a bit, Grandpa Foster wants to have a word."

"Shirley, Shirley, a few days ago I had the strangest of dreams; but things are starting to make some sense at last. Listen! I felt as if I had been transported back into another world in the time of slavery. A man was there and the numbers....*465 465 465 465*.....kept running through my mind so I couldn't see beyond the fog that was around me, and neither could I move. There was a big gate closed in front me and you were all there too."

"Then I saw this butterfly and suddenly Ananse appeared. It was like watching a drama, and afterwards the fog lifted. I began to make sense of some experiences and remembered things I haven't thought of for years... the heroes that were recognised after we left Jamaica, all the ones that stood up against the oppression of slavery and the stories momma used to tell me. Stories like this must be across the lands affected by the atrocity."

"You know we used to talk about going home after five years of being in England for our real freedom. Where is home? How far back do we go? I have not shared the nightmares that have often gone through my mind in the past. Sometimes this has bothered me so much."

At this point the Sankofa bird began directing his thoughts, concerned that the image of *465* might appear again. But there was no need to worry, Mr. Foster had the message and continued, "You know, I never wanted to talk about the time of slavery. I held back to get through life, and put it of my mind. But that's because I was only hearing one story."

"Yes," Shirley agreed. "Your grand children said the right things at the school today. This is our real freedom, wherever we are; listening to the young people talking like that, and all of us working together across the oceans to support the building of a new equilateral structure. Our dreams are being fulfilled in front of our eyes!"

Mr. Foster spoke confidently, "We must not let anything stop us from valuing our rich history and culture, and using our talents and skills to make this world a better place. Strength lies in collective communities, in doers not just talkers. It's too easy to blame the other person and use excuses not to do things; or hurt others when you can't catch the real culprit who may be more powerful than you. 'If yuh kyaan ketch Quacko yuh ketch im shirt.' Do you remember that?"

"Yes, I do," answered Shirley. "So we have to stand up and work together, be proud of who we are and proud of the real heroes who paved the way before us. In the same way Ananse's web and the Sankofa bird take us back to the past to remind us and forward to the future where there is a place for all of us."

"Shirley, we must be prepared to raise our voices when we know things are not right, that way change will happen. You know my brother in Jamaica, your Uncle Barry? He used to share stories with me about life in Jamaica just before independence. He did some important things there during that time. I'll talk to you again very soon about more of this."

Mr. Foster passed the phone back to his wife. "We have so many different stories to share, and experiences that have affected us all in so many different ways." She said to Shirley, "We have to talk together, don't just hide feelings or pretend to be alright and look good on the outside."

"Yes, thank you. I've got to make some more calls now. See you soon Momma." Shirley hung up the phone and then dialled her uncle's number in Jamaica.

"Uncle Barry, wappn? It's me Shirley. You won't believe the things that have been happening to us over here. We all have so many different stories to tell, and we must remember the journeys we have taken. Even when we reach positions of power we must consider the experiences of others and work together for the betterment of all mankind. I know you did that. Jamaica's National Anthem created for our country's independence in 1962 sums it up..... 'Justice, Truth be ours for ever, Jamaica land we love.' " She explained what the youngsters had done and said that she wanted to bring them over to Jamaica for a visit.

"Do it," Barry agreed. "There are so many places we could take them to. Remember my son lectures at the University and there are going to be some special presentations going on at my grand daughter's school. We miss you all. Come soon, I'll start making plans. We all need to play our part. Remember... 'Every mikkle mek a mukkle' "*

*Every little bit counts

Aisha went home and picked up the phone to make her regular call to her mother. "Mommy, you would have been proud of me in the assembly today. We led the programme an mi big up Jamaica a whole heap! Mi know tings nah easy fi yuh, but we have a lot to be thankful for. Many of those who made a difference in the past came from difficult situations and that made them more determined to do something to make change happen. I told everyone I'm going to be a scientist and do things to make the world a better place. Mi a go mek yuh proud!"

Similar empowered conversations went on in many other families when the pupils went home. Phone lines were busy across the country and the oceans, sharing and understanding each other's experiences and coming up with creative ideas to move forward.

SHACKLES
AND
WEBS

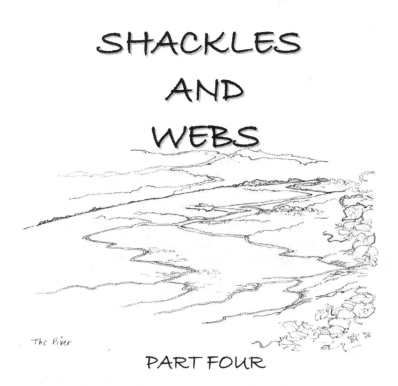

The River

PART FOUR

Together

Ananse heard all the conversations through his contacts on the web. He moved on to the branch of a tree near the school hall and smiled a smile as wide as the reflection of the golden gates that were visible, and wide open, shining through the school window.

That night he called the animals together for a meeting in the nearby forest.

"Bees, you build your own hives to make honey. Birds your nests are great and we use the same trees as you for our webs. I know we don't always get it right but it is better when you own your own place, choose your own career and run your own business. Then we can all see our dreams at the end of the rainbow. Tiger keep away!"

He shook all his legs in harmony with his speech and the community of creatures realised what Ananse was trying to do.

The bees buzzed, "Now we understand what you were doing, Ananse, when you asked us to help you to get Tiger to stop being so selfish. Thank you. Now we know our job is not finished, there are so many real stories to spread around."

The choir of bees joined together to rehearse their songs and discuss their flight plans and itinerary. They could envisage the new life reviving each congregation when they presented the message to them. In many places people seemed happy with their lot in life, but that was often a coping strategy and the creatures wanted to sing to them the real songs of freedom.

"Nuh tan deh an look; join in de play," they buzzed.

"Hol on, no badda go wey right now. A whole heap o sinting a jus gowaan! Mi wan put dem inna new story. Listen, an tel mi how it stay. Truth yuh tel dem." Ananse exclaimed.

The butterfly flew down and perched on the

branch close to Ananse where he could see the animals gathered.

"Crick", he said.

"Crack," the animals replied.

"Dis a wah gowaan," Truth continued.

"It was the year 2007. The people said it was the Bicentenary of the abolition of the transatlantic slave trade. Two hundred years before they had passed a Parliamentary Bill to abolish the slave trade in what they then called the British Empire."

"Ananse did hear dis pon im web, an im vex, big time! Listen to what im did sey...."

" 'Lawd a mercy, a lie dem a tell!' Mi neva see im so vex. Im eye watta an all o im eight leg a tremble." Truth continued to tell the story.

"Ananse did call mi an tell mi a whole heap o sinting. Firs im say transatlantic slavery neva done fi another 30 years or more after 1807, in sum places 60 years; an odda form of slavery still happenin right now! Den im sey a whole heap o sinting nah deal wid yet! People nah get treated fair cos o dem colour. In sum places people nah ave nuttin an don noh wah fi do. If dem kyaan reach who dem wan fi reach some o dem a cus and hurt dem brudda."

He took a deep breath. "Den, sum o de pickney dem nah do good in school. An im sey Tiger tief a whole heap o im story agen an nah tellin dem right. It a mess tings up big time!" Truth paused and

81

spoke powerfully, "Ananse said he was going to something about it. He turned to me and said, 'Truth, mi need yuh help. Get unnu wings workin good, mi ave sinting fi yuh to tek somewhere fi mi.' "

"Then he gave me some letters with _465_ written on them. Im sey, 'Dis a fi mi bigges ginnal act. Deliva dem inna de minds o de people on dis list.' He gave me a paper with some names on. He continued, 'but watch cos Tiger a do de same kind o sinting an mi nah wan im fi know dat mi a stir it up more fi a reason.' "

Truth sighed, drew a deep breath and explained, "Mi fly like mi neva fly before, all ova de place. Den mi kom to Ananse's name on de list. Mi call im an sey, 'Ananse, sinting nat right, why yuh name here?' "

" 'Mi know wah mi a do. Gi mi de letta nah!' Ananse said. Then he went on to his web and fell asleep."

"I flew over and delivered the letter into his mind. That's when everything started to happen. The message in the letters stirred up the past, and something seemed to make people think in a way they had never felt before. Ananse chose special people to deliver the letters to. At first it hurt, but then when the past was dealt with, they were stronger, and acted to make a difference. And up 'til now Tiger doesn't know we double tricked him."

Ananse joined in, "Yes, Truth, an mi nah finish yet. Mi a go strengthen mi web inna de sky cos mi need sum more Spiritual power fi do mi nex job across mi web on de earth. Sum o de time dem big up mi ginnal character too much an miss de message. Mi need fi pass de wisdom on to de people dem. De Sankofa bird a go help mi too."

"Jackmandora," he stated.

"Mi nah choose none," said Truth who then flew off to finish his job.

Ananse returned to his web in the school ceiling. It felt stronger as he moved across the fibres. The thought streams of the children, their families and members of the wider community trickled slowly into an ever widening river.

AKOMA NTOSO: Linked hearts
Understanding and agreement

Alongside the river another landscape was developing. Ananse felt his web rising to a new height. The rafters in the school ceiling were being replaced by the image of a mountain peak. The replacement structure was being born with a unique equilateral profile.

The young people could be seen climbing up one face, their mountaineering equipment grabbing enthusiastically into the rock.

Around the corner Miss held on tightly and the sides grew stronger as their joint determination strengthened the evolving shape.

The parents and grandparents heard the voices

and felt their children's determination pulling them to another side of the structure.

As they all rose to new heights the Sankofa bird joined Ananse on the peak and they watched the new rivers beginning to flow down the mountain, invigorated by the joint energy.

From the peak the view was amazing. The group then realised they were not alone. There was a whole assembly of people from diverse backgrounds and experiences across the Diaspora, who had reached the summit; and there was room for everyone. They were equal, and united in purpose, determined that the new structure should come into fulfilment.

Refreshed by rain from heaven the rivers continued their flow into the sea of life. The energy soon began to reach distant shores, spreading the powerful messages. This included the reality that those who profited in the past, and continue to do so, should play a major role in supporting the growth of this new equilateral structure.

This role should not be just a one off apology, but the development of sustainable opportunities for the lands and the descendants of those affected by the Transatlantic Maafa. An environment where everyone can see a place for themselves and achieve their potential must be the ultimate goal.

MPATAPO: Knot of reconciliation
Peacemaking and reconciliation

As this new landscape was being born another scene was evolving. Several hundred miles away in a remote corner of the English countryside a Mercedes Benz was pulling up to a large golden gate in front of a mansion.

An elegantly suited gentleman was pressing desperately on his car horn whilst listening to the busy sound on his mobile phone. The gate house was unoccupied and the golden framework in front of him was locked tightly.

Tomorrow was going to be another hard day. There was a pile of paperwork and decisions to be made around the table with his colleagues, and he wasn't ready for them yet!

He had been given a list of concerns to address following the recent celebration of the Bicentenary of the Abolition of the Transatlantic Slave Trade. The items on the list related to the economies of the countries involved, poverty in certain areas and unemployment. It also included statistics about rising crime rates in some areas, particularly involving young men; and the underachievement of children in the education system. He had been advised to link with others in the various countries to analyse the reasons behind the problems and decide on the way forward.

"That's their problem. What has this got to do with me? Transatlantic slavery was over a long time ago!" He thought, and honked furiously on his horn once more!

There was still no response and he quickly climbed out of the vehicle to check the lock on the gate post. A fresh spider web clung to the chain around the frame.

As he walked up and raised his hand towards the lock a butterfly flew over his head.

The sunshine at this exact moment sent a beam of light like an arrow directed at its target. The lock shone brightly and the numbers...*465 465 465 465*...flashed in front of the man's eyes. He closed them quickly, in confusion, and further figures, behind closed bars, marched like a regiment after the flashing numbers.

Subsequently, a voice spoke through the silence.....

"In some places
We're still livin' in a tenement yard.
As the old are dying
The youth are aspiring.
Within the rotting boards
And aging zinc
The dreams still flourish.

What's happening?
Keep the spirit, the family united,
Give real Freedom,

Support the dreams to fulfilment
Or nightmares will continue."

The gentleman tried to dismiss the scene with little success. He lifted his head and peered once more through the gate. The huge mansion house, passed on to him by his father, stared at him like a mask.

Suddenly a cloud of mist floated around his ankles, under the gate and over towards the mansion. With surreal energy the historical structure rose upwards, propelled by the swirling mist.

As the mist cleared, the foundations of the mansion were revealed. Shackle shapes were flying around on the landscape of an old sugar plantation.

The clattering shackles gradually changed form as they rose out of the plantation. Empowered by the financial energy, cogs and machinery took over and the Industrial Revolution began.

At this point the mansion house began a new life and various characters started walking in and out of its doors. Each one was well dressed and powerfully moving on, head held high, to destinations of confident purpose.

The figure at the gate was following the scene in front of him. He glanced back at the foundations where the old sugar plantation lay. Within the mist he saw other figures struggling to rise, strong and determined; they were looking for the way forward.

Many of them moved on confidently, joining the others walking out of the doors; but others seemed to be trapped in the mist and the remaining shackles. The scene was bewildering.

Once again he heard voices echoing through the silence.

"Rhatid! Rhatid! Rhatid! Raaaaaa!!!" The emotions of anger and powerlessness resonated helplessly through the mist. A single voice rose higher exclaiming…………

"Rhatid! "

Wrath internalised boasts
Revs beyond a Ferrari,
Poised at the starting line
But never moving.
Power boosting uncontrollably
'Til the engine bursts into flames
And dies,
Taking with it
All those around in its furnace.
Rhatid!

Heal the wounds,
Harness the creative power
Behind Rhatid
And the world is
Your race track.
Know your vehicle,
Fill with healing oil,
Keep your eyes on the road, and
Weaving through and round the obstacles
You pass the finish line
With a rosette of honour.
Victory!

RHATID - 'wrath'. [anger, often with a desire for revenge]

Gradually the mist began to clear and the mansion house settled again on its foundations.

Looking back at the lock on the gate the inheritor of the mansion house heard a click; the gate opened, and Truth the butterfly flew over his head. The spider's web seemed to suddenly expand and he saw eyes gazing at him through the maze.

He climbed into his car once more and drove through the entrance. At the side of the driveway he saw a fresh stream flowing down from the hillside. He had never noticed this happening before and there had been no recent rainfall. As the water flowed new thoughts began racing through his mind. He watched the scene before him.

REMNANTS

Gentle ripples of water
Touched on the banks of the stream
Running down from the mountain.
The regular rhythms
Reverberated through the air,
Slush…sh…sh,
As if voices were talking under the surface,
Propelled by a soft, calm breeze
In the twilight hours.

Darkness fell like an illusive cloak.
Slush…sh…sh, it's me, me, me,
Continued mysteriously through the shadows.

90

Shackles and Webs

At the sunrise
A hand reached out from the darkness
And pulled the cloak off the night.

The eyes of a tiger
Glowed in the shadows
Fighting the daylight,
With conflicting messages.

The banks were littered with
Remnants cast aside from the historic flow.
A stick of oppression,
Torn bags of troubles,
Broken branches of the family tree,
Lost childhood wrapped in a broken baby doll,
Pieces of Bling, Bling blinding reality,
Racist mindset locked in a coconut,
Splintered identity,
Poverty trapped in a broken fishing net,
Achievement ambushed by pirate fisherman
and
A cracked shell, empty of heritage.

Footsteps were heard
Crunching through the sand
Accompanied by the sounds
Of a sweeping broom.
Ripples of sand unfolded
Moved by the strokes of the broom.

The bristles touched upon
Pieces of a shattered mirror.
The worker placed them together

Like a jigsaw
And viewed his face in wonder as if seeing it
Complete for the first time.

Considering the remnants in a new light
He made decisions about each one.
Brandishing his broom with a fresh energy
He began to….
Recycle,
Reclaim or
Scrap, scrap, scrap.

Soon the individual brushing sound
Turned into an orchestra of creativity
As others joined in…
Retell,
Remodel
Repair or
Renew, renew, renew.
More brushes and materials arrived,
Delivered from higher up the stream
And the mountains
'REDEMPTION.'

The stream continued,
Refreshed by the new energy,
And freed from the remnants littering its banks.
The voices turned into a choir
Singing in tune with the instruments
in the orchestra
'FREEDOM!'

Shackles and Webs

The observer continued driving up to the door with the thoughts still dashing through his mind. As he came close a bird flew onto the step. The Sankofa bird looked backwards and caught his eye. Then the gaze of the bird changed direction, pulling him forwards. He looked up at the framework of his inheritance in a new light.

In a few moments he was sitting down at his desk and the task ahead suddenly felt no longer like a burden but an urgent responsibility. Creatively he drew up plans to channel the financial energy behind the task he had been given, into areas where it was really needed. To do this effectively he realised that he needed to listen to the voices of the characters at the base of his vision; both the ones who confidently moved on and those who seemed trapped. Then he had to work together with all of them to plot the new paths.

For the first time he grasped his pen with a new energy he had never felt before. The structure of the mansion was no more a safe haven of rest but a power to be harnessed into making a difference. He realised that he needed to spread this message to others in power for them to realise the truth.

At this moment the scene moved back to the mountain top carrying the observer with it. He was no longer alone and felt the presence of others who were singing a song in perfect harmony, accompanied by a unique orchestra. Through the shadows he could make out some familiar faces from his recent visions and realised that he had

93

joined a choir.

Gradually, his eyes became accustomed to the ambience. He was able to see the new landscape with Ananse and the Sankofa bird standing on the peak.

Suddenly he saw Ananse swing over on a strand of his web and land at his side. A butterfly was with him and together they were holding a paper. They passed it to the observer. He found his part and joined in, no longer an observer; singing the song of Freedom.

The Sankofa bird moved his head in rhythm with the new song and dived into the clear water at the spring. He began shaking his feathers as he plunged and released energy from the past. Playing in tune with the dancing ripples the ancestors powerfully joined in the chorus.

At last the tides were filled with faith and hope and the potential gained strength to heal the wounded and enrich the far corners of the earth. The voice of Truth echoed through the shadows reminding everyone of the dream that should not be forgotten......

'With this

FAITH

we will be able to hew out of

the mountain of despair

a stone of

HOPE.'

'From every mountainside let

FREEDOM

ring.'

'FREE AT LAST'

THANK GOD ALMIGHTY

WE ARE FREE AT LAST.'*

*Martin Luther King

A
Rainbow
shone through to reveal the beginning of...

The River

REAL
EMANCIPATION

Further links...

www.jamaicabicentenary.org.jm
Our Freedom journey: Honouring our Ancestors through publications, activities and Diaspora links.

www.emancipationpark.org.jm
"Freedom to Hope, to Excel and to Be." Emancipation Park is dedicated to highlighting the history, culture and flora of Jamaica. The park's design and statues celebrates the island's emancipation from slavery.

www.antislavery.org/breakingthesilence
A site that aims to support educators to break the silence surrounding the transatlantic slave trade and help people to move forward.

www.setallfree.net
Project of Churches together in England.

www.promotingourheritage.com
Promoting our Heritage: Increasing access to spoken and written material about Jamaican Heritage.

www.garveylibertyhall.com
The legacy of Marcus Garvey.

www.swagga.com/marcus.htm
Declaration of the Rights of the Negro Peoples of the World.

www.jcdc.org.jm
Jamaica Cultural development Commission.

www.blackpupils.com
An innovative educational resource for black pupils, teachers and community groups.

www.blackhistoryfoundation.com
Experiences of black people are an integral part of mainstream Britain, not to be sidelined or devalued.

www.bbc.co.uk/history/british/modern/arrival
Windrush passengers tell their stories.
www.tidec.org TIDE Global learning
- JAMAICA - 'Out of many one people' poster pack.
- Exploring Ubuntu / Towards Ubuntu.
- Learning today with tomorrow in Mind
www.swagga.com
Great Kings and Queens of Africa
www.welltempered.net/adinkra
West African Wisdom: Adinkra Symbols &
Meanings. The Akan of Ghana make exclusive use
of a system of symbols. Each symbol is associated
with a proverb or saying rooted in the Akan
experience.
www.africaresource.com
Educational arts and research programmes....
The Global Black Inventors Research Projects Inc.,
President - Keith Holmes
www.africawithin.com/tour/ghana/kente
History and significance of Ghana's Kente_cloth.
www.banyan.uk.com
Banyan products: Eric Pemberton. Setting up and
running a successful school Wari Club.
www.usconstitution.net/dream
Martin Luther King's dream.
www.officialkwanzaawebsite.org
Kwanzaa – The first fruits of the harvest.
www.bobmarley.com
Bob Marley, his life, his music, his legacy.

"Mi tel yuh aready, mi a go strengthen mi web inna de sky cos mi need sum more Spiritual power fi do mi nex job across mi web on de earth. Den mi can pass de wisdom on to de people dem. De Sankofa bird a go help mi too. "

"Mi soon kom wid more stories fi tell yuh, from people livin cross mi web. Watch dis space!"

THE AUTHOR: Mary Nelson

Mary spent her teenage years in the 60's growing up in Bristol amongst the Caribbean community where her father was a pastor. Because of her own diverse history she was very sensitive to the racism and inequalities in established systems, and the wider community that were affecting her friends and their families who were otherwise actively involved in her father's church. Following these experiences she decided to train to teach with a focus intent on equality for all.

Her employment began in Wolverhampton in the early 1970s as class teacher. This was in a primary school during a time of extreme racial unrest and inequality for minority ethnic children and communities. Her class had a high number of new arrivals from India and the Caribbean. She confidently involved parents and community in her practice, developing the curriculum with the children in the centre.

From there she taught in a similar situation in inner London and made plans to go to Jamaica to experience the culture and learn more of the history. She began to teach in Kingston in 1973 and also became involved in various Arts, and community activities. She attended Bethel Baptist Church where she taught in JAMAL adult education classes and joined the gospel choir. It was there she met her husband who had a similar vision in his own life and career.

Links with these organisations, Education, the

University and the Creative Arts in Jamaica has formed a foundation for ongoing Projects today… valuing Jamaican culture and language, and building links with Britain.

Mary spent several years in the USA in a management role where she also was aware of inequalities in the corporate scene and education systems.

She returned to England to teach in the West Midlands, again with a focus on equalities. She then held a management role, in the Equalities and Diversity Service. In this position she was actively involved in local and national projects to support raising the attainment of underachieving groups.

She continues to support her husband in his Caribbean Cuisine, music, and other business projects where together they hold on to their unique vision and value their joint heritages. They are currently supporting the family in developing their own businesses based on the same unique foundations and vision they have passed on to them.

Mary has now established an educational consultancy.....**'Sankofa Directions'.**

Learn from the past in building the future
www.sankofadirections.com

THE ILLUSTRATOR: Andrew Hazel

Andrew is fortunate to be able to work at what he loves – Art and English. As a secondary school teacher he takes a creative approach to teaching and learning that is as much fun as it is challenging and academic. As a freelance illustrator he has worked on several projects around culture, black history and raising awareness of historical and contemporary issues.

Darees Nelson

Darees is the author of 'Things have changed,' and formatted the cover illustrations by Andrew Hazel.